WAUKAZOO ELEMENTARY LI

Z0040306 FIC PAU
WILD CULPEPPER CRUISE
Paulsen, Gary.

S0-AFV-043

DATE DUE

OCT 28 2003
APR 12
APR 20
NOV 15 2006
MAY 4 2011

The Wild Culpepper Cruise

OTHER YEARLING BOOKS YOU WILL ENJOY:

THE VOYAGE OF THE *FROG*, *Gary Paulsen*
THE BOY WHO OWNED THE SCHOOL, *Gary Paulsen*
THE COOKCAMP, *Gary Paulsen*
THE RIVER, *Gary Paulsen*
THE MONUMENT, *Gary Paulsen*
HOW TO EAT FRIED WORMS, *Thomas Rockwell*
HOW TO FIGHT A GIRL, *Thomas Rockwell*
HOW TO GET FABULOUSLY RICH, *Thomas Rockwell*
SHILOH, *Phyllis Reynolds Naylor*
SOUP IN LOVE, *Robert Newton Peck*

YEARLING BOOKS/YOUNG YEARLINGS/YEARLING CLASSICS are designed especially to entertain and enlighten young people. Patricia Reilly Giff, consultant to this series, received her bachelor's degree from Marymount College and a master's degree in history from St. John's University. She holds a Professional Diploma in Reading and a Doctorate of Humane Letters from Hofstra University. She was a teacher and reading consultant for many years, and is the author of numerous books for young readers.

For a complete listing of all Yearling titles,
write to Dell Readers Service,
P.O. Box 1045, South Holland, IL 60473.

WAUKAZOO SCHOOL LIBRARY

Gary Paulsen

The Wild Culpepper Cruise

CULPEPPER ADVENTURES

A YEARLING BOOK

Published by
Dell Publishing
a division of
Bantam Doubleday Dell Publishing Group, Inc.
1540 Broadway
New York, New York 10036

If you purchased this book without a cover you should be aware that this book is stolen property. It was reported as "unsold and destroyed" to the publisher and neither the author nor the publisher has received any payment for this "stripped book."

Copyright © 1993 by Gary Paulsen

All rights reserved. No part of this book may be reproduced or transmitted in any form or by any means, electronic or mechanical, including photocopying, recording, or by any information storage and retrieval system, without the written permission of the Publisher, except where permitted by law.

The trademark Yearling® is registered in the U.S. Patent and Trademark Office.

The trademark Dell® is registered in the U.S. Patent and Trademark Office.

ISBN: 0-440-40883-0

Printed in the United States of America

November 1993

10 9 8 7 6 5 4 3 2 1

OPM

The Wild Culpepper Cruise

Chapter • 1

Amos was out of breath. He had forgotten his bicycle and had run all the way to Dunc's—Duncan Culpepper's house.

He pounded on the front door.

Mrs. Culpepper opened the door. "Hello, A—"

He raced past her and up the stairs to Dunc's room.

"Amos." She shook her head. "Strange boy."

He burst through the bedroom door.

Dunc was reading the *Stock Market* journal. For once Amos didn't notice Dunc's overly neat room. He usually hated neat. Neat bothered him. But not today.

"You'll . . . never . . . guess!"

Dunc sat up. "Calm down, Amos. Catch your breath."

Amos Binder was Dunc's lifetime best friend. Dunc was used to his strange behavior.

Amos took a deep breath. "You'll never guess what happened. Go on—try. Take a guess. Any guess. You won't guess in a trillion years. Well, go on—guess!"

Dunc thought about it. "From the way you're acting, I'd say . . . you won something."

Amos's face fell. "You guessed. How did you do that? I come over here with the best news of the century. The most exciting thing that will probably ever happen to me in my entire life, and instead of waiting for me to tell you—you guess."

"I'm sorry, Amos. You told me to guess."

"Okay. So you know I won a contest. But you don't know what prize I won, do you? Just try and guess that! Go ahead!"

"You got me. I don't know."

"Aha! I knew you couldn't guess. Get ready. Here it comes. Are you ready?"

"I'm ready already. What?"

Amos danced around in a little circle. "A cruise. I won a cruise—in the Caribbean. Can you believe it?"

"That's really great, Amos. When do you go?"

Amos stopped dancing and put his hands on Dunc's shoulders. "That's the other great news. The cruise is in two weeks. It's a seven-day cruise for four people. My sister Amy can't go because she has cheerleading camp."

Dunc looked puzzled. "I don't understand. Why is that great news?"

"Get with the program, Dunc. Count: My dad. My mom. Me—and you. Four people."

A smile touched the corner of Dunc's mouth. "Me?"

"Of course you, dummy. Who else?"

Dunc beamed. "A trip to the Caribbean. Who'd ever have thought we'd wind up there?"

Amos took a travel brochure out of his pocket and spread it out on the bed.

"Here's a picture of the ship. It's *The Lady Anne,* with Duchess Cruise Lines. We go to a lot of islands, and to part of Mexico. Everything is paid for, except souvenirs and junk."

"Amos, how did you do it?"

"What?"

"Win. What did you do to win? You never even told me you were entering a contest."

Amos folded up the brochure. "I don't always tell you everything. Almost everything. Not everything."

"Tell me how you won the cruise."

Amos looked down at the floor. "I wrote an essay for a dog food ad."

"And?"

"And it won."

Dunc cleared his throat. "Let me get this straight. You wrote an essay about dog food and won a cruise. That's it?"

Amos nodded. "Actually, I was trying for the bicycle. But the cruise will do."

"What did you write about?"

"You had to ask, didn't you?" Amos sat on the edge of the bed. "The title was the same for everybody who entered—'My Dog, Why I Love Him.' "

Dunc stared at him. "Amos, you *hate* your dog! You and your dog have never gotten along. You try to give him away every chance you get. And Scruff hates you too. He bites you every time he sees you."

"Details. The rules never said what you

wrote had to be true. If they assume that—well, that's their problem. I won fair and square because of my ability to write believable fiction. Anyway, it's about time that dog was good for something."

"If you say so, Amos."

"I say so. That dog doesn't know it yet, but because of him I'm going to overwhelm Melissa."

"How do you figure that?"

"When she sees my island tan and finds out I'm a world traveler, she's bound to be impressed."

Melissa Hansen was the girl Amos loved. He adored her, but she didn't know he existed. He spent half his life trying to get her attention. Somehow, he never quite got it.

Amos stuffed the brochure back in his pocket. "I think she tried to call me again yesterday. I'm pretty sure it was her. I have her ring memorized."

Dunc nodded. He knew Melissa wouldn't be caught dead calling Amos. But he never told Amos that.

"It didn't work out too well, though. She really shouldn't call me when I'm at the dentist."

"She called you at the dentist?"

"Yeah. But like I said, it didn't work out so hot. I was leaning back in the chair, and Dr. Fulbright was filling a cavity way back here." Amos opened his mouth to show Dunc the tooth.

"Anyway, he had the light in my face, like he always does, and that little table over me with all his tools and stuff. Lisa—she's the new dental assistant—she was sucking up the spit in my mouth with that sucker thing, when I heard the phone."

"What made you think Melissa was calling you at the dentist's office?" Dunc asked.

"It surprised me too. I don't know how she knew I was there. Maybe she followed me or something. But it was her ring, all right."

"What happened?"

"Well, naturally when I knew it was Melissa, I jumped out of the chair to answer it."

"Naturally," Dunc said.

"I accidentally hit the tray of dental tools, and they flew up into the light. One long silver thing got stuck up in there. They got the fire out pretty fast, though."

"Fire?"

"That long silver thing made a lot of sparks.

They flew around the room and caught the fake plant in the corner on fire. It was really more smoke than fire. A lot of the patients thought it was a real fire, though, and ran outside hollering. But that's not the bad part."

"There's more?" Dunc asked.

"Dr. Fulbright didn't get the drill turned off, and he drilled right through his new dental chair. While he was doing that, Lisa got the spit sucker caught in his hair. I always thought that was his real hair. Didn't you?"

Dunc nodded.

"By the time I made it out to the receptionist's desk, Melissa had already hung up. She likes for me to get it on that all-important first ring. She doesn't like to wait."

Dunc nodded again.

"Dr. Fulbright asked my mom if we would please find a new dentist. I really hate to see a grown man cry like that."

"Amos, you're amazing."

"What? Oh, you mean because I won the cruise. Yeah, sometimes I even amaze myself." Amos headed for the door. "Well, I have to go. I'll be back later to help you pack."

"Where are you going?"

"I need to get home. Melissa may have heard about the cruise by now. She's probably been trying to call."

Dunc smiled.

Chapter · 2

"I can't believe it. We are actually standing in the Miami airport. Tomorrow we'll be cruising around in the Caribbean. It's unreal. What's the name of the hotel we're staying at tonight?" Dunc asked.

Amos was watching the luggage carousel go around. "I don't remember. It's one of those big ones. The Tilton, I think."

"There's mine." Dunc grabbed his suitcase.

"I wonder where mine went. I tied one of Amy's new red hair ribbons on the handle so I'd be sure and recognize it."

"It'll turn up. Be patient. We have plenty of time. Your folks went to see if the cruise line sent a car for us."

"There it is," Amos said. "No wonder I didn't see it before—the ribbon came off. Oh, well. Let's go find my parents."

The ride was a blur. The driver of the minibus broke land speed records getting them to the hotel.

Amos's dad tried to get him to slow down so they could see some of Miami, but the man did not understand English. Mr. Binder attempted to ask him to slow down in Spanish, but it came out, "Please, sir, can I have a drunk tortilla?"

The driver looked at him strangely and went even faster.

When they arrived at the hotel, the driver put the luggage on the sidewalk and took off at something close to the speed of light.

Amos craned his neck to see the top story of the hotel. "Wow! I hope our room is on the very top."

Their rooms were on the fifteenth floor. It wasn't the top, but it did have a balcony overlooking the ocean.

Amos threw his suitcase on the bed. "Come on. Let's look this joint over."

Dunc was carefully hanging his clothes in the closet. "In a minute. Let me get unpacked."

Amos had always thought Dunc was too organized for his own good. He turned on the TV and plopped onto the other bed. The news was on. A reporter was telling about a robbery that had taken place in Fort Lauderdale earlier this morning.

"I'm glad we only stopped in Fort Lauderdale to change planes," Amos said. "Those guys look mean."

Dunc was hanging up a T-shirt. He leaned over to see the television. "They're ugly too. Look at that one. He has a scar down the side of his face. I'd sure hate to meet him in a dark alley."

Dunc closed his empty suitcase and put it in the closet. "Okay. Let's go."

They headed straight for the top of the hotel, where they found a swimming pool and a Jacuzzi. The view of the ocean was spectacular. It was blue as far as you could see.

"Let's go get our trunks on," Amos said. "This pool has my name on it."

They rode the elevator back down and raced the length of the hall to their room.

A tall, extremely thin man was bent over the

door to their room. When he saw them, he turned and walked quickly around the corner.

Dunc grabbed Amos's arm. "Did you see that?"

"What?"

"That man was trying to break into our room."

Amos made a face. "Give it a rest. You're not solving any mysterious crimes on this trip. The guy probably works for the hotel."

"I don't know. He sure acted funny."

"Lighten up. This is a vacation. Save all that detective stuff for when you get home." Amos unlocked the door. "Last one in the pool is maggot food."

He grabbed his suitcase. It was locked. "That's funny. I know I didn't lock it. I don't have a key."

Dunc tried to open it. "Go see if your mom has a hairpin or something we can use to get it open."

Amos ran across the hall and came back with a long hairpin. He wiggled it in the lock until it popped open.

"Oh."

"What's wrong?" Dunc asked.

Amos stared in the suitcase. "This isn't my stuff."

"You must have grabbed the wrong bag at the airport."

"What do I do now?"

"You search it and see if you can find out who it belongs to." Dunc picked up the phone. "I'll call the airport and see if they have your bag."

The clothes obviously belonged to a man. Whoever owned the bag was traveling light. Everything was brand-new. A new set of clothes, new shaving supplies, and a newspaper.

Dunc put the phone back down on the receiver. "The airline doesn't know what happened to your suitcase. They're going to check on it. And no one from our flight has reported theirs missing. Did you find any identification?"

Amos shook his head. He picked up the suitcase. "What am I supposed to do with this?"

"The guy at the airport said to hang on to it until he gets back to you."

"When exactly is that going to be? We're leaving in the morning. What do they want me to do? Wear the same sweaty clothes for seven days while I drag some strange man's stuff all over the Caribbean?"

Chapter · 3

"It's a good thing you let me hold our tickets," Dunc said.

"I wish my parents had let you hold theirs. Then they'd be here instead of racing back to the hotel to get them," Amos said.

Dunc looked at his watch. "They'll be here. They've still got forty-five minutes. While we're waiting, let's look around the ship."

Amos turned around and bumped smack into a little girl.

"I'm sorry. Did I hurt you?"

The little girl straightened her dress and

smoothed her long hair. "No, I'm perfectly fine, thank you."

Amos started to walk away. She pulled on his sleeve. "My name's Vanessa. What's yours? I'm five years old. I go to school. I can write my whole name, and I can count to one thousand without stopping. What's your friend's name? I have a cat. Her name is Amanda. We play house. Do you like to play house?"

Amos looked at Dunc. He patted Vanessa on the head. "We have to go now. 'Bye."

Vanessa grabbed his sleeve again. "I have to stay right here. My mommy said I can't go anywhere. She wants me to wait for her. You can wait, too, if you want. I have a doll. When my mommy gets back, I'll ask her if I can show my doll to you."

Amos uncurled Vanessa's fingers from his sleeve. "I'd really like to see your doll, but I need to go. Now."

Dunc laughed. "Does Melissa have competition?"

"Don't be dumb."

They walked out on one of the decks. People had already changed to bathing suits and were sitting by the pool sipping drinks with umbrellas stuck on top.

The ship was a floating entertainment center. It had its own gambling casino, movie theater, stage show, three lounges, a banquet hall, shuffleboard, volleyball, video game room, skeet shooting, and mini–shopping mall.

They wandered from room to room exploring. A woman in a blue sailor suit gave them a list of the classes that would be offered aboard ship. They could choose from painting, karate, aerobics, snooker, dancing, snorkeling, and shooting.

Another woman gave them a schedule of floor shows, movies, and sight-seeing tours.

"Didn't I tell you it was going to be great?" Amos said.

Before Dunc could answer, an announcement came over the ship's loudspeaker.

"All nonpassengers will please leave the ship at this time. Once again, all nonpassengers are asked to disembark at this time. We are about to set sail."

Dunc looked at his watch. "Oh, no. It's time! Let's find out if your parents made it—come on!"

They raced down the narrow hall to the boarding area.

"I don't see them anywhere," Amos said.

A small hand tugged on Amos's sleeve. When he looked down, he saw Vanessa smiling up at him. "What's the matter, boy? Did you get lost from your mommy?"

"No—yes. Well, sort of."

"If you get scared, you can stay with me."

"Thanks, Vanessa. Not right now. I need to look for my mommy—uh—mom."

The ship started to pull away from the dock. People were screaming and throwing streamers and confetti.

Amos stared at the shore. "How could this have happened?"

Dunc looked around. "Don't worry. They're probably on board somewhere. Let's go check their cabin."

Another announcement came over the ship's loudspeaker: "Will passenger Amos Binder please report to the main deck."

They climbed back up the stairs.

"I don't see them," Amos said.

A woman with a clipboard walked over. "Are you Amos Binder?"

Amos nodded.

"Someone wants to speak to you on the ship-to-shore telephone. Would you follow me, please?"

Chapter 4

Amos sat on his bed in the cabin. He rested his chin in one hand. He let out a long sigh and then shifted to the other hand.

Dunc sat on the other bed and watched him.

"Cheer up, Amos. It's a bad deal that your folks got left behind, but it's not the end of the world. When they called, they said to go on and have a good time."

Amos looked at the floor.

"Let me put it another way," Dunc said. "We have seven days on a luxury cruise in an island paradise without any parental supervision."

Amos sat up. A grin spread across his face. "Hey, that's right. We don't have anybody to answer to. We can do whatever we want." He frowned and slumped back on the bed.

"Then why do you still look so sad?"

"I don't feel so hot. I wish this ship would quit rocking." Amos ran for the bathroom. After a few minutes he yelled through the door. "I'll just live in here. You go on and have a nice cruise."

"Don't be silly, Amos. I'll go up and see if I can get you some pills for seasickness. Don't go away."

"Very funny."

Dunc locked the door behind him. He took the stairs two at a time. In the mini-mall he found a box of pills, paid for them, and started back down the stairs to their cabin.

A tall, thin man was walking down the hall toward him.

Dunc stared at him.

The man lowered his head and kept on walking.

Dunc ran for the room. "Amos. It's him! The same man from the hotel. He's here on the ship."

Amos's face had a greenish tint. "Did you get me some pills?"

"Oh, yeah—here." Dunc handed him the box. "Did you hear what I said?"

Amos gulped the pills and leaned back on the bed. "What are you babbling about?"

"The man. The skinny one at the hotel. He's here. On this ship," Dunc said.

"So? It's a free country. Probably half the people who stayed in that hotel last night are on this ship."

"Don't you think it's strange that he keeps coming around to our room?"

Amos shook his head. "Maybe his room is down this hall."

Dunc stared out the window.

"Please don't do that," Amos said.

"What?"

"Look like that. That look means trouble. Listen, there is absolutely no reason for that man to be interested in us. So get it out of your head."

Dunc snapped his fingers. "Right. You're right, Amos. He would have to have a reason to be interested in us."

He pulled Amos's look-alike suitcase out of

the closet and poured everything out onto the bed.

"We've already searched it. What do you think you're going to find this time?" Amos asked.

"I don't know. But that man is interested in us, and I want to know why." He carefully examined each item except for the few clothes Amos had managed to buy at the hotel.

Everything in the suitcase was new. Even the newspaper was only two days old.

The newspaper.

Dunc yanked it out and started reading. It was a Fort Lauderdale paper. There were several stories on the front page. The one that caught his eye had two pictures below the headline.

"That's it, then." Dunc sat on the edge of the bed. "At least now we know who he is."

"Who?" Amos grabbed the paper.

Dunc pointed at one of the pictures. "That's the guy. I should have recognized him from the news story on TV."

Amos read the headline. " 'Pair wanted in connection with robbery.' " He looked up. "These guys stole a half-million in jewels. We're getting into serious stuff now. Are you sure it's the same guy?"

Dunc nodded. "I'm positive. But there's something I can't figure out. Why would they go to so much trouble to get this suitcase back? There's nothing in it . . . or is there?" He tore the top edge of the lining loose and felt inside.

"What are you doing? You can't go around ripping up other people's suitcases."

"I've seen this trick on TV. Crooks sew stuff in the lining of their suitcase to get it through customs." Dunc shoved his hand all the way to the bottom of the lining.

"I hope you know what you're doing," Amos said.

Dunc put the suitcase down. "I don't understand it. There's nothing here."

"It's a good thing you didn't tear up the clothes and the shaving stuff, or we wouldn't have anything to give back to the airline."

"Of course." Dunc grabbed the shaving bag. He unzipped it and dumped the contents onto the bed: a razor, a can of shaving cream, and a bottle of aftershave.

He unscrewed the cap on the aftershave and

carefully poured it into a glass. Then he drained the liquid out of the glass.

"Look at this." Dunc gave the glass to Amos.

It was full of sparkling jewels.

Chapter 5

"If you have one of your brilliant plans, now would be a good time to let me in on it," Amos said.

Dunc poured the jewels from one hand to the other. "Well, we can't go to the police. There aren't any. About the only thing we can do is hide the jewels and do our best to stay away from the thieves until we get back to Miami."

"That's a plan? That's not a plan. I could have come up with that."

Dunc shrugged. "Here." He gave Amos some of the jewels. "We'll each take half. Now all we have to do is make sure we stay around a lot of other people. They won't try anything in a crowd. When we get back, we'll go to the police. Simple."

"Simple? The paper said these guys were dangerous. Do you understand what that means?" He went on before Dunc could answer. "It means we could end up as shark bait."

Dunc stuffed his half of the jewels into his pocket. "Let's get something to eat. I'm starving."

"How can you think about eating at a time like this?"

Dunc opened the door a crack and looked out. "All clear. Come on, Amos. We're on vacation. Let's try and have a good time."

Halfway down the hall Amos felt someone touch his arm.

"Aahhh!" He jumped backward.

"Hello, boy."

It was Vanessa.

"I was looking for you, boy. My mommy said I could show you my new doll. Where have you been, anyway? I had the hiccups last night and kept everybody up until midnight. Where are you going?"

She stopped talking and stuffed a piece of caramel candy into her mouth.

"I've got things to do, Vanessa. You know . . . ah—letters to write and stuff." Amos looked around. "Where's your mommy?"

"My mommy's resting. My nanny is watching me today."

"She is? Where? I don't see her."

Caramel dripped down the corner of her mouth. She giggled. "My nanny is pulling the handle of that machine with the fruit. It goes around and around. She really likes to do that. One time she let me pull it, and a whole bunch of silver pennies came out."

Amos cupped his hand to his ear. "I think I hear your nanny calling you."

Vanessa skipped off down the hall toward the casino.

"Looks like you have an admirer," Dunc said.

"You know me." Amos held out his arms. "Everywhere I go, women fall at my feet."

They climbed two flights of stairs and walked out on deck.

Dunc took a deep breath. "Doesn't that ocean air smell great?"

Amos looked out at the water. It was dark

blue, almost black. The waves lapped up against the side of the ship with a gentle rocking motion.

He held his stomach. "You go ahead and eat. I'll stay here and keep this rail company."

A huge buffet of food encircled the swimming pool. There was a three-piece Jamaican band playing at one end. Dunc piled food onto his plate and carried it back to Amos.

Amos took one look at the food and heaved over the rail.

"Do you feel better now?" Dunc asked. "You still look a little green."

"Thank you so much for telling me."

"Just trying to help."

"Go help someone else. I was doing just fine without you."

Dunc looked over the side. "It's a good thing there's not much of a breeze. Otherwise the people on the deck below might come up here looking for you." He plopped a big strawberry into his mouth.

Amos closed his eyes. "If you are through being helpful, I would appreciate it very much if you would go somewhere else to feed your face."

"Are you sure you're not hungry?" Dunc looked down at his plate. "These little fish wimming in this brown gravy look pretty ood."

"Go!"

Dunc started to walk away when Amos rabbed his arm.

"Would you make up your mind? Do you ant me to stay or not?"

"Shh," Amos whispered. "Try not to be too bvious. Look at that guy standing by the door."

Dunc turned his head.

It was the other man from the newspaper—he one with the long scar down his face.

Dunc set his plate on a table. "Let's see if we an get out of here without being noticed."

They inched toward the stairs.

"Hello, boy."

Amos knew who it was before he turned round.

"Vanessa," Amos whispered, "I'm busy right ow. I've got some grown-up things to take care f. You be a good girl and go play."

She whispered back, "Who's a grown-up?"

"She's got you there," Dunc said.

Amos flashed him a hostile look. "I think our nanny's calling you again, Vanessa."

She looked at him suspiciously. "Are you ure?"

He nodded his head.

The minute she was around the corner, they took off running. When they reached the door of their room, Amos fumbled in his pocket for the key.

"I don't think you'll need it." Dunc said.

The door was open a couple of inches. He pushed it the rest of the way.

The room was in shambles. Everything had been dumped out, torn up, or thrown on the floor.

Chapter · 6

The sun was shining through the small round porthole in their room. Dunc was already up brushing his teeth.

Amos yawned. "What time is it?"

"Time for you to get up. We're going to miss the sight-seeing tour of Chichén Itzá if we don't hurry."

Amos yawned again. "Chicken pizza?"

Dunc came out of the bathroom. "It's pronounced *che-CHEN-eat-za.* Chichén Itzá. It's an ancient Mayan Indian city."

Amos rubbed his eyes. "Ancient Indians ate pizza?"

"Never mind. We're docked at Cancún. The bus leaves in thirty minutes. Hurry."

They had to run to catch the last of the three tour buses. It was large and comfortable, with sliding windows and seats that lay back. Dunc took pictures of the Mayan villages out the window.

Amos took a nap.

"Wake up, Amos. We're here."

"Already?" Amos stretched. "I'm really beat. I didn't get much sleep last night because stayed up and watched the door."

"You could have gone to sleep. We were safe enough. We put a chair under the doorknob and piled anything that would move in front of it."

"I know. I was part of what we piled in the chair, remember?"

A tour guide was waiting outside their bus. He was a friendly-looking man with a stubby beard.

"Good morning. And welcome to the famous Chichén Itzá ruins. If you will follow me, we'll begin our tour at the ball courts."

Amos scratched his head. "Ancient Indians played ball?"

The tour guide smiled at him. "Yes, they did. The game was like a mixture of basketball and soccer. See the high rings on either side of the court? They had to get the ball through those without using their hands. They literally played for their lives. The ill-fated captain of the losing team also lost his head."

"That must have been some game," Dunc said.

The guide let the people look around for a while. Then he called them together to move on to the next spot.

"The next stop is the Sacred Well. It is the site of countless human sacrifices. The unfortunate victim would be purified in a steam bath and would then either jump or be pushed from that stone platform."

Amos shuddered. "They sound like real nice people."

Dunc was taking pictures. He focused his camera on a tour group standing on the other side of the well.

He quickly looked up.

"Amos, we may have a little problem here."

"What's the matter?"

"They're here."

"Who?"

"Scarface and Skinny. They're on the other side of the well. Remember our plan. Stay close to people."

Amos decided to glue himself to the tour guide. The man couldn't turn around without stepping on him or bumping into him.

When they reached the temple, the guide encouraged everyone, especially Amos, to climb the seventy-five feet to the top.

"Come on, Amos," Dunc said. "Let's go with this group."

"No, thank you. I'd rather stay down here with our trusty tour guide."

"Amos, give the poor guy a break. Come on."

"Oh, all right," Amos snapped. He turned to the guide. "I'll be right back."

The man gave him a halfhearted smile and waved. "I can't wait."

The group moved slowly up the steep face of the pyramid. At the top was a square door that led to the main room. The room was filled with ornate carvings of birds and animals. A large stone altar sat near the wall in the front.

"Stand by the altar, Amos. I want to get your picture."

Amos moved over to the altar. First he just stood by it, but then his ego took over and he really started posing. He sat on it, then lay on it with his arms folded, eyes closed, and tongue hanging out. They were so busy with the pictures, they didn't notice their group go on to the next room.

Amos was showing Dunc a tiny lever he'd found on the back of the altar when another tour group started to filter in.

The two men saw them right away and started toward them.

Amos looked up. Right into the eyes of Scarface. He lost his balance and fell against the lever.

The altar moved. A loud scraping sound filled the room. Where the altar had been was a black hole.

Amos could feel himself falling. He grabbed Dunc's arm. Together they fell into the seemingly bottomless hole.

It was a slide.

They landed in a heap at the bottom. It was nearly pitch black, and for a moment they could see nothing. Then their eyes became accustomed to the darkness and Dunc grabbed Amos by the arm.

"Come on."

"Where?"

"We're at the bottom of the pyramid. It must have been a secret escape route the priests had in case they needed to run. There's a side tunnel over here. . . ."

He dragged Amos along, and in a few moments they came out in bright sunshine, almost in the middle of the main group of tourists.

Chapter 7

"Come on, Amos. We can't stay cooped up in our cabin for the rest of the trip."

"This wasn't my first choice. I wanted to stay inside the bottom of that pyramid. It was a good safe place. But no. You had to find the way out and insist we come back here. I think you enjoy playing hide-and-seek with those crooks."

"We'll be safe as long as we stay around other people," Dunc said. "Come on. We'll go up and find some kind of class to take. It'll be good for us to get our minds off our problem for a while."

Amos sighed. "Okay. But only if I get to choose the class."

They made their way up to the recreation deck. Most of the classes had already started.

"Are you boys looking for something to do?" A young man dressed in the ship's blue uniform smiled at them.

"We were looking for a class to take," Amos said. "But it looks like we're too late."

"I happen to know one that hasn't started yet. Come with me." He led them down the stairs to one of the lounges. A band was playing.

"Here we go." The young man motioned for the instructor to come over. "This is Roberto. He's our dance teacher." He turned to Roberto. "These boys would like to be in your class."

"I—I'm not too sure about this," Amos stuttered.

A teenage girl came over and took Dunc's hand. "I need a partner. Do you mind?"

Amos was trying to back out the door. He backed right into a short, plump woman.

She squealed, "Oh, goody! A partner."

Amos looked around. "Who, me?"

She pulled him onto the dance floor.

Roberto carefully explained the steps to the

next dance, but Amos wasn't listening. He was glaring at Dunc. "I'll get you for this."

The band started playing. The first dance was a fast polka. The woman danced while Amos ran wildly, trying to keep up. He would have slipped out the door on one of the turns, but she had a death grip on his arm.

They made two complete circles around the room to everybody else's one. Each time around she screamed in his ear, "Isn't this fun?"

By the time the music finally stopped, Amos was so dizzy he fell to the floor.

Roberto blew a whistle and told them to change partners.

Now's my chance, Amos thought. He crawled for the door.

"I believe this is our dance, sonny."

A gray-haired lady pinned him in the corner with her walker.

Amos looked up at her. "I think I'll sit this one out."

"Eh? What'd you say, sonny?"

He stood up, got close, and yelled, "I'm too tired from the last one!"

She cackled. "You want a fast one? Me too, sonny. Let's go." She grabbed his ear and pulled him along.

The dance was a slow one. Which was good because the old lady could barely walk, much less dance. And she never let go of his ear.

Amos looked around for Dunc. He finally spotted him sitting on a bench in the corner.

Of course, Amos thought. I'm getting my ear ripped off, and he sits over there without a care in the world.

Fortunately the song was a short one. When it was over, Amos headed straight for Dunc.

"I hope you're having a good time."

Dunc nodded. "I'm doing okay. How about you?"

It was on the tip of Amos's tongue to tell him exactly what kind of time he was having. But he never got the chance.

The leanest, meanest, biggest woman Amos had ever seen in his life spun him around. She made a Mack truck look like a Tonka toy.

"I ain't got nobody to dance with. *Get over here!*"

"Uhhh . . ." Amos squeaked.

When the music started, she grabbed him and locked him in position. Amos tried to reach her hands, but it was impossible. She was so big, he could barely touch the ends of her fingertips.

She danced like a cougar with rabies, throwing Amos around with the beat of the music, flipping him in the air. With the final fanfare from the band she bounced him clear across the room where he hit a marble column, glanced off, and headed for Roberto and the band.

Roberto sidestepped neatly, and Amos went headfirst through the bass drum.

Chapter • 8

Amos shook his head. "I'm not going. This trip is jinxed. Every time I leave this room, I throw up, get chased, fall down a black hole, or land in a drum." He folded his arms.

"This time it'll be different. We'll just take a quiet stroll on deck. Maybe play some shuffle-board or something."

"You say that, but it won't turn out that way. Those crooks are probably just waiting for us to come out."

"Have it your way," Dunc said. "I hope it doesn't get back to Melissa, though."

"What?"

"If she finds out you spent most of your time in the cabin, I doubt if she'll be very impressed."

"She won't know," Amos said.

"I thought you were going to overwhelm her with your island tan."

Amos thought about it. "I guess it would be a shame to waste what little time we have left shut up in this stuffy cabin."

Dunc nodded.

"Okay. I'll give it one more try." He held up his finger. "But *only* because of Melissa."

It was a beautiful day. The sun sparkled on the ocean. A fresh saltwater scent filled the air.

Amos squinted in the bright sunlight. He held his hand up to protect his eyes. "Okay. You got me up here. Now what?"

"You name it," Dunc said. "We'll do whatever you want."

A strange look came over Amos. "Anything?"

"What exactly did you have in mind?"

"How much money do you have left?" Amos asked.

"A little. Why?"

"I've been thinking of trying my luck at the slot machines."

"Amos, you don't have any luck, and besides, you can't go into the casino unless you're twenty-one or with an adult."

"It figures. I knew I should have stayed in the cabin."

Dunc sighed. "Oh, all right. I think I know how to get you in. Follow me and do what I do."

Dunc led the way to the casino. He stood outside the door watching the people go in and out.

"What are we waiting for?" Amos asked.

"I'm looking for the right . . . shh! Here he comes now."

A short, bald man in a yellow and brown plaid leisure suit walked up to the door.

Dunc fell in behind him. He motioned for Amos to follow.

The casino attendant started toward them.

Dunc said in a loud voice, "Okay, Dad, we'll wait for you over here by the slot machines."

The attendant turned and went back to his position by the door.

"You play," Dunc said. "I'll keep an eye out for trouble."

Amos played hard. He shoved one coin in after another. He came close a couple of times, but he never won.

"Give it up. You're going to break me." Dunc grabbed his arm. "Let's go find something else to do."

Amos put in another coin.

"Hello, boy."

He turned around. Vanessa and her nanny had walked in. She ran over and proudly handed him her new doll for his inspection.

"I named her after you."

Amos took the doll. "I didn't know you knew my name."

"I don't. What is it?"

"But I thought you said . . ."

"It's Amos," Dunc interrupted. "Amos Binder. I think that was a very nice thing for you to do, Vanessa. He's honored. Aren't you, Amos?"

"Yeah. Honored." He tried to hand the doll back.

Vanessa held up her little hands. "You can hold her awhile if you want. She likes you. I can tell. Do you want to play house? You be the daddy, and I'll—"

Amos stood up and laid the doll on the stool. "I have to go now, Vanessa. But I'll tell you what. You can pull the handle of this machine and keep anything that comes out."

He hurried across the room. Dunc waved at her and followed.

When they reached the door, a loud siren went off. Amos turned around.

Vanessa had pulled the handle and hit the jackpot. Silver coins crashed down around her. She giggled and clapped her hands. Then she picked up one of the coins and ran over to Amos. She stuffed it in his hand and gave him a big hug.

"Thank you, Amos! You're my very best-est friend."

Chapter • 9

"It's a good thing we dock in Miami tomorrow," Amos said. "I can't wait to get off this dumb ship."

Dunc was making his bed. "Are you still mad about Vanessa and the money?"

"That and everything else. It's not fair," Amos sulked.

"You're the one who told her she could keep anything that came out of the machine."

"Don't remind me. I was so close to being filthy rich. Think of it. Money—combined with my charming personality. Melissa would have been powerless. She was within my grasp, and I blew it."

"Amos, you don't want Melissa to like you for your money."

"I don't?"

"You're hopeless." Dunc sat on the end of the bed. "I've been thinking."

"Uh-oh."

"Cut that out. This is important. We dock tomorrow, and the crooks still don't have the jewels."

"I thought that was the idea," Amos said.

"It is. But don't you think it's strange that they haven't tried very hard lately?"

"Maybe they decided to give up and go straight."

Dunc shook his head. "I don't think so. I think the reason they haven't bothered us is because they have something big planned for tonight."

"Are you trying to tell me that our last night on this dumb ship is going to be the worst?"

Dunc smoothed out a wrinkle on the bed. "I hope not. But we need to be prepared just in case."

Amos dragged the chair across the floor and started piling things on it.

WAUKAZOO SCHOOL LIBRARY

"What are you doing?"

"Getting prepared. Isn't that what you said to do?"

Dunc smiled. "You don't need to do that. I've figured out a way to keep the jewels safe and get the crooks off our backs."

"I should have known." Amos sat down. "Well, let's hear it."

"Tell the captain."

"Right. And just how are we supposed to do that? He's driving the ship. No one except the crew is ever allowed to see him."

"I know that. But I also know that tonight is the captain's banquet. I read it on the schedule. The last night of the cruise, the captain gives this big formal banquet. He shakes hands with the passengers and eats dinner with them."

"Why don't we give the jewels to one of the crew?" Amos asked. "They could give them to the captain, and we'd be out of it."

"Who can we trust? Whoever we give them to might take off with them. No, we have to get to the captain."

"What are you [illegible]?"

[illegible] that [illegible] you said [illegible]

Dunn smiled. "You don't need to [illegible]. I've figured out a way to keep the jewels safe and out [illegible]."

"I [illegible] have [illegible] down well [illegible] the captain."

"Again. And just now we [illegible] supposed to [illegible] thing. No one [illegible] ever allowed [illegible]."

"I know that. But [illegible] know the [illegible] captain's [illegible]. I [illegible] the last night of the [illegible], the captain gave [illegible]. He shook hands with [illegible] Jones with them."

"[illegible] the jewels [illegible]," [illegible] said. "They would [illegible] the captain [illegible] out of [illegible]."

"When [illegible] What [illegible] them [illegible]. We [illegible]."

[illegible]

Chapter · 10

"How do I look?"

Amos was admiring himself in the mirror. He had been to the mini-mall and purchased a bright purple bow tie. It was the kind with sparkly elastic that went around the neck.

He had chosen to wear a red and yellow Hawaiian-style shirt, along with jeans and high-tops.

His hair was dripping. He had it slicked all the way back.

Dunc looked him up and down and tried to

keep from smiling. "I bet you'll be the center of attention."

"Thanks." Amos straightened his bow tie. "Are you ready?"

Dunc buttoned the cuff on his white shirt. "I think so. Do you have your part of the jewels?"

"Right here." Amos patted his pocket.

"Well, we'd better go then. We don't want to miss shaking hands with the captain."

Dunc turned the doorknob. Nothing happened. He pulled on it. Shook it and yanked hard.

It wouldn't open.

Amos tried. He braced himself against the wall and pulled with all his might.

The door wouldn't budge.

"Looks like they got to us before we could get to them," Dunc said. "I should have guessed they'd try something like this."

"You think the crooks locked us in here?" Amos looked alarmed.

"Who else? Pretty smart. This way they know we're not going anywhere. They can come get the jewels anytime they want."

Amos let it sink in. Then he started banging on the door. "Help! Somebody help us!"

"You can save your breath. By now, they're

all upstairs at the banquet. Nobody's going to hear you." Dunc lay back on the bed.

"Now is not the time for a nap!" Amos yelled. "We have to do something."

Dunc sighed. "There isn't anything to do. They've won. We'll have to hand over the jewels. They won't hurt us as long as they get what they want."

Amos turned around and stared at him. "Duncan Culpepper. I don't believe it. You're giving up. You're feeling sorry for yourself because they out-thought you."

"I am not. I'm facing facts. There's obviously no other way. . . ." He looked up. "Hmmm?"

He stood on the bed and opened the small porthole and looked out. "Look, Amos. The main deck isn't too far from our room."

He moved so Amos could look.

Amos quickly pulled his head back in. "Are you crazy? There's nothing out there to stand on except air."

"Didn't you see that cable? It's connected solid to the side of the ship, and it runs all the way around to the deck."

Amos looked again. "That tiny wire? Not this boy! No way!"

"You're probably right." Dunc lay back down

on the bed. "We'd be better off to stay here and wait for them to come after us. It would have made great headlines though—'Daring Boys Elude Jewel Thieves.' "

"How about 'Boys Drown While Being Stupid on Pleasure Cruise,' " Amos said.

"It doesn't make any difference to me if we stay or go," Dunc said. "You're the one I was thinking of."

"You want me to drown?"

"No, of course not. I wanted you to get the credit. Our hometown paper would be bound to carry the story. Melissa would read it, and—"

Amos broke in, "And it wouldn't matter that I'm not filthy rich. I'd be a hero. She'd be awe-struck."

He started out the porthole.

Chapter · 11

"Are you sure this thing will hold us?" Amos asked.

"Wrap your leg around it just in case. Mountain climbers do that. That way if they slip, their leg catches them."

Amos moved an inch at a time. The deck was still a good ten feet away. "I sure am glad it's dark."

"Why?"

"That way I can't see how far it is down to the water."

"It's about a two-story drop," Dunc said.

"Thanks. I needed to hear that. It's much easier knowing that if I fall, I'll have time to die of a heart attack before I drown and get eaten by sharks."

"Nobody's going to drown. We're almost there. Only a few more feet to go."

Amos groaned and moved a few more inches. "By the time we make it to the banquet, it'll probably be over. The captain will be in bed, and this will all be for nothing."

"No, these things go on all night. They never eat right away. They talk and make all kinds of introductions first."

"I've reached the end, Dunc. Now what?"

"This is going to be the tricky part. You have to let go with one hand, grab the rail, and swing up. Be careful."

Dunc heard a ripping sound. "What was that?"

"My pants. Watch that bolt as you swing up."

Dunc swung up behind him. "We made it. Are you okay?"

"Except for my pants. I'm sort of exposed in the back."

"We don't have time to go back to our room." Dunc looked around. He pulled a red-striped cloth off a deck table. "Here. Put this on."

Amos tied it in a knot around his middle. "I can't wear this. It looks like a dress."

"You look fine. Come on."

The banquet hall was crowded. Most of the people were dressed in formal evening clothes. The crew wore their dress uniforms.

Everything about the room was elegant. Chandeliers hung from the ceiling. Delicate ice sculptures of dolphins and various fish sat on each table. Food was stacked everywhere.

Dunc shook his head. "Three countries wouldn't be able to eat all the food here."

When Amos walked in, he heard a small ripple of laughter. He looked down at himself. His bow tie was crooked. He straightened it and hitched up the tablecloth.

"I thought you said I looked fine," he whispered.

"Don't worry about it," Dunc said. "Help me find the captain."

Hundreds of people were standing around in small groups talking. It was hard to see.

"There he is." Dunc pointed to a group of women standing around an officer. They made their way through the crowd. Everyone they passed stared at Amos.

He stared back. "It's the latest thing. Your

kids will all be wearing tablecloths soon. Wait and see."

The captain was surrounded by layers of people. Dunc tried to elbow his way in, but it was impossible.

Amos didn't try. He decided to stop at the dessert table and sample at least one of everything. The choices were almost endless. He started with a piece of five-layer chocolate cake. Then ate his way down one side of the table. At the other end he was about to reach for a strawberry parfait when he happened to look up.

Skinny and Scarface were on the other side of the table.

Amos looked around for Dunc but couldn't find him. He stepped back and started to run—or tried to. But he tripped on his tablecloth and fell into a woman carrying a glass of punch. It went down the front of her dress. She screamed.

He tried to stand up. Scarface reached for him. Amos dodged and fell backward onto the end of the dessert table. The other end came up and sent cakes, pies, and ice cream flying through the air.

The five-layer chocolate cake went straight into the ceiling fan. Pieces splattered all over the room. The floor was a slippery mess. People were screaming and sliding into each other.

Amos crawled under the drink table. He thought he was safe until an arm reached for him. Reflexes took over, and he tried to stand up. All of the crystal glasses and a huge silver punch bowl went crashing to the floor.

Amos crawled out on the other side of the table.

Above all the noise and confusion he thought he heard Dunc's voice. He looked up. Dunc and the captain were waving to him from the kitchen door.

He frantically scrambled to his feet and ran for the kitchen. When he got there, Dunc grabbed him and pulled him down behind the stove.

The two crooks ran in after him. They looked at the chef and the waiters. Scarface growled, "Did you guys see a kid come in here?"

Everybody in the kitchen pointed at the big walk-in freezer. The crooks looked inside. The captain and some of the waiters came up from behind, shoved them in, and locked the door.

[illegible] in. The floor was a [illegible]. People were screaming and slamming into each other.

As it crashed against the [illegible] table, the punch bowl [illegible] reached [illegible] the [illegible] were [illegible]. All the crystal glasses and a large silver punch bowl that contained the punch.

[illegible] crashed and [illegible] on the [illegible] of the table.

Above all the noise and confusion he thought he heard the [illegible]. He [illegible] and the captain were starting to [illegible] from the [illegible] door.

He finally pulled himself to his feet and ran to the [illegible]. When he got there, [illegible] grabbed him and pulled him [illegible] the deck.

[illegible]. They looked at the [illegible] and the [illegible] [illegible] you see a [illegible] and [illegible]

[illegible] the [illegible] pointed at the [illegible] [illegible] the [illegible] and some of the [illegible] [illegible] he [illegible] the [illegible]

[illegible]

Chapter · 12

"There's no place like home." Amos slam-dunked a dirty sock through the hoop on his door.

"We've been home for over a week. When are you going to quit saying that? You sound like Dorothy in *The Wizard of Oz*."

"I can't help it. I'm glad to be back. No seasickness. No jewel thieves chasing us. It's great. Hey—what happened to those guys anyway? I hope they got frostbite."

"No such luck," Dunc said. "The Coast Guard was nearby. They came out right away and picked them up. The captain handled everything. He even arranged for your parents to go on the next cruise."

"Yeah, I guess he's okay. I wish it had been our picture in the paper instead of his, though."

"He was the one who thought of trapping them in the freezer. And after the mess we made of his ship, we're lucky he didn't give us to the Coast Guard."

Amos made a long shot with another sock. "I guess you're right. I heard him say something about us and the *Titanic.*"

"Oh. I almost forgot." Dunc reached into his pocket. "Your mailman brought this package."

"Stick it on my desk. I'll give it to my parents when they get back."

"It's addressed to you."

Amos grabbed the package. "It's from Vanessa. How did she get my address?"

"Open it," Dunc prodded.

"There's a letter with it." He cleared his throat. " 'Dear Mr. Binder. I am writing this letter on behalf of my charge, Princess Vanessa.' " He looked up at Dunc. "Princess Vanessa?"

"Read the letter."

" 'Her Grace would like to thank you for your kindness toward her aboard ship. The money you gave her will be given to a charitable cause in our country. Enclosed is a drawing done by the princess. She would also like for you to have this silver fountain pen, due to the excessive amount of letters you write. She hopes you will think of her when you use it.' It's signed, 'Sincerely, Princess Vanessa Elizabeth Dumont of Cervina Bosnio.' "

"How about that." Dunc grinned. "Vanessa is a princess."

"A princess who took all my money," Amos said.

"What did she draw?" Dunc asked.

Amos pulled a stiff piece of paper out of the envelope. It was a stick-figure drawing of Amos, Vanessa, and her doll.

Dunc looked over his shoulder. "It's a perfect likeness."

"Cute," Amos said. He ripped open the box. "Look at this pen, Dunc! I think it's real silver."

"That Vanessa must be really special," Dunc said. "It's not often that people go to so much trouble. Especially someone as young as she is. You'll probably treasure that pen for years and years. It makes you feel good. Kind of restores your confidence in people, doesn't it?"

Amos dropped the letter and headed for the door.

"Where are you going?"

"To see how much Eddy Sanders will give me for a solid silver pen. Where else?"

Dunc grinned. "Like I said, it restores your confidence in people."

Be sure to join Dunc and Amos in these other Culpepper Adventures:

The Case of the Dirty Bird

When Dunc Culpepper and his best friend, Amos Binder, first see the parrot in a pet store, they're not impressed—it's smelly, scruffy, and missing half its feathers. They're only slightly impressed when they learn that the parrot speaks four languages, has outlived ten of its owners, and is probably 150 years old. But when the bird starts mouthing off about buried treasure, Dunc and Amos get pretty excited—let the amateur sleuthing begin!

Dunc's Doll

Dunc and his accident-prone friend, Amos, are up to their old sleuthing habits once again. This time they're after a band of doll thieves! When a doll that once belonged to Charles Dickens's daughter is stolen from an exhibition at the local mall, the two boys put on their detective gear and do some serious snooping. Will a vicious watchdog keep them from retrieving the valuable missing doll?

Culpepper's Cannon

Dunc and Amos are researching the Civil War cannon that stands in the town square when they find a note inside telling them about a time portal. Entering it through the dressing room of La Petite, a women's clothing store, the boys find themselves in downtown Chatham on March 8, 1862—the day before the historic clash between the *Monitor* and the *Merrimac*. But the Confederate soldiers they meet mistake them for Yankee spies. Will they make it back to the future in one piece?

Dunc Gets Tweaked

Dunc and Amos meet up with a new buddy named Lash when they enter the radical world of skateboard competition. When somebody "cops"—steals—Lash's prototype skateboard, the boys are determined to get it back. After all, Lash is about to shoot for a totally rad world's record! Along the way they learn a major lesson: *Never* kiss a monkey!

Dunc's Halloween

Dunc and Amos are planning the best route to get the most candy on Halloween. But their plans change when Amos is slightly bitten by a werewolf. He begins scratching himself and chasing UPS trucks—he's become a werepuppy!

Dunc Breaks the Record

Dunc and Amos have a small problem when they try hang-gliding—they crash in the wilderness. Luckily Amos has read a book about a boy who survived in the wilderness for fifty-four days. Too bad Amos doesn't have a hatchet. Things go from bad to worse when a wild man holds the boys captive. Can anything save them now?

Dunc and the Flaming Ghost

Dunc's not afraid of ghosts, although Amos is sure that the old Rambridge house is haunted by the ghost of Blackbeard the Pirate. Then the best friends meet Eddie, a meek man who claims to be impersonating Blackbeard's ghost in order to live in the house in peace. But if that's true, why are flames shooting from his mouth?

Amos Gets Famous

Deciphering a code they find in a library book, Amos and Dunc stumble onto a burglary ring. The burglars' next target is the home of Melissa, the girl of Amos's dreams (who doesn't even know that he's alive). Amos longs to be a hero to Melissa, so nothing will stop him from solving this case—not even a mind-boggling collision with a jock, a chimpanzee, and a toilet.

Dunc and Amos Hit the Big Top

In order to impress Melissa, Amos decides to perform on the trapeze at the visiting circus. Look out below! But before his best friend for life, Dunc, can talk him out of his plan, the two stumble across a mystery behind the scenes at the circus. Now Amos is in double trouble. What's really going on under the big top?

Dunc's Dump

Camouflaged as piles of rotting trash, Dunc and Amos are sneaking around the town dump. Dunc wants to find out who is polluting the garbage at the dump with hazardous and toxic waste. Amos just wants to impress Melissa. Can either of them succeed?

Dunc and the Scam Artists

Dunc and Amos, best friends for life, are at it again. Some older residents of their town have been bilked by con artists, and the two boys want to look into these crimes. They meet elderly Betsy Dell, whose nasty nephew Frank gives the boys the creeps. Then they notice some soft dirt in Ms. Dell's shed, and a shovel. Does Frank have something horrible in store for Dunc and Amos?

Dunc and Amos and the Red Tattoos

Dunc and Amos head for camp and face two weeks of fresh air—along with regulations, demerits, KP, and inedible food. But wherever these two best friends go, trouble follows. They overhear a threat against the camp director and discover that camp funds have been stolen. Do these crimes have anything to do with the tattoo of an exotic red flower that some of the camp staff have on their arms?

Dunc's Undercover Christmas

It's Christmastime! and Dunc, Amos, and Amos's cousin, T.J., hit the mall for some serious shopping. But when the seasonal magic is threatened by some disappearing presents and Santa Claus himself is a prime suspect, the boys put their celebration on hold and go under cover in the perfect Christmas disguises. Can the sleuthing trio protect Santa's threatened reputation and catch the impostor before he strikes again?